The dia
A MEDIEVAL SQUIRE

D0824034

WITHDRAWN

For Jack

Editor Louisa Sladen
Editor-in-Chief John C. Miles
Design Billin Design Solutions
Art Director Jonathan Hair

© 2003 Franklin Watts

First published in 2003
by Franklin Watts
96 Leonard Street
London
EC2A 4XD

Franklin Watts Australia
45-51 Huntley Street
Alexandria
NSW 2015

ISBN 0 7496 4895 3 (hbk)
0 7496 5158 X (pbk)

A CIP catalogue record for this book is available
from the British Library.

Printed in Great Britain

The diary of A MEDIEVAL SQUIRE

by Moira Butterfield

Illustrated by Brian Duggan

ALLEYN'S SCHOOL
THE FENNER LIBRARY
942.03
CLASSIFICATION

FRANKLIN WATTS
LONDON • SYDNEY

ALL ABOUT THIS BOOK

This is the fictional diary of William De Combe, a sixteen-year-old boy living in medieval England in 1332. He is a squire, living at the manor of his uncle, Sir John De Walton. One day he may become a knight, but first he must undergo training.

A KNIGHT'S TRAINING

AGED 7 TO 8

A boy such as William, the son of a knight, was sent to another nobleman's house to be a page. He would learn skills such as archery and hunting, reading and writing.

AGED 15 TO 16

At this age a page became a squire. He would be trained to fight and to look after his master's weapons and armour.

AGED 18 TO 24

During this time a squire might be knighted himself.

MEDIEVAL ENGLAND

Medieval England was a feudal society, which means it was organised in strict order of rank. This is how it worked:

The king was the ruler.

Important nobles (**earls** and **dukes**) were given land by the King in return for providing fighting men when needed.

Knights were given land by the nobles. In return they fought for the nobles for a number of days every year.

Freemen rented land from knights. In return they fought for their knight when they were asked to do so.

Villeins farmed small strips of land for themselves but they also worked for the owner of the estate they lived on. They might be asked to fight for him, too.

6 JUNE 1332
THE MANOR OF WALTON

There is a small bird fluttering high up among the wooden rafters of the hall. I can see the sharp shadows it makes in the firelight, flickering this way and that across the stone wall. Everyone else in the hall is asleep except me. The pages, the dogs and servants are all slumbering in corners. It would be completely peaceful except for the bird and the sound of my quill pen gently scratching on parchment.

Earlier it was all harrumphing and grumbling, when my uncle, Sir John De Walton, came stomping through, moaning about a bad day's hunting and an "infernal toothache".

I wasn't quick enough. He saw my quill pen quivering in my hand.

"William! You're scratching words again! You're a squire, boy, not a scribe! How old are you? Sixteen? You're not some page who needs

to practise his letters. Or perhaps you're writing love poetry, eh?"

"No Sire, I am not!" I blushed as others in the hall laughed. Sir John seemed about to snatch my words and read them out, but he turned away when my aunt, Lady Eva, appeared.

"There is word from Piers De Montald," she said in her quiet, determined voice. Sir John instantly forgot about me and disappeared up the stairs behind her to the solar room, a clear sign he wanted to speak to her privately.

It was a close call. I can see that if I want to write undisturbed I must only do it by candlelight when the others are asleep, as I do now, or I must do it in a private hidden place. Sir John does not understand why I waste my time writing and in truth, even I do not know why I have always loved to fill a piece of parchment with my thoughts. Cousin Isobel says that it is probably because my mother first taught me my words, putting her hand over mine to help me hold the quill.

7 June 1332

Bayard's huge back is steaming in the sunlight that slants through the door of the stables. I have brushed his coat and fed him. Now my tasks are done, I can sit behind his silent bulk so no one can see me from the courtyard and the manor buildings beyond. I can pull my writing tools from their new hiding place behind the feedsacks, and I can write privately amid the hay and horses.

Bayard has turned his head and is looking at me with his huge inquisitive eyes. He is so big that his head alone is as long as my outstretched arm. He is worth a fortune to Sir John, as much as if he had precious stones for eyes. "Sir John is a great fighter. He needs a strong mount. You won't find a finer fighting horse than Bayard," Adam always says.

Adam was here in the stable a few minutes ago. He doesn't tease me about my writing. He can't read anyway, but he knows a lot besides words. Since he was born in the village and has been a manservant to my uncle forever, he must know every blade of grass and stone in this place. Unlike me, he has followed my uncle to battle and I remember him telling me that after a charge Bayard's eyes roll around and he seems to blow smoke like a magic creature.

It has been a while since Sir John has been called upon to fight for the King, not since he took a bad wound in his arm against the Scots. And not since I was made a squire last year. Now his arm has healed, but, according to Adam, the enforced rest is why my uncle is so prone to grumpiness.

"Sir John is a fighting man to his bones and he misses it," Adam insists. "The sight of his sword knocks the very breath out of any enemy. As for the tournament; there he is master of all. You shall see."

"Will I? When?" I asked excitedly, but Adam only winked and smiled.

He knows a secret. I can tell. I think he just whispered it into Bayard's flicking ear.

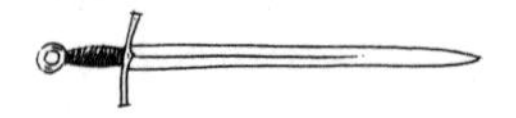

8 JUNE 1332

At dawn, Uncle John clattered down from the solar and swept through the hall, his big bellowing voice scattering the dogs under the tables.

"Where is my squire? Ah, there you are, boy. We have work to do! I will practise with the lance at the quintain and with the rings, too. Saddle up Bayard. Is my armour clean? It had better be!"

His face was lit by a grin but when Lady Eva came scuttling up behind him I thought she had shadows around her eyes that weren't there yesterday. She protested quietly: "Sir John, you are to meet the reeve and the bailiff today. There are estate matters to decide."

Sir John swerved round, crestfallen. "Oh... yes. That must be done, I suppose. Well, we will practise in earnest tomorrow. Now come up to the solar, boy."

He still calls me "boy", my great bellowing

uncle, though I am already sixteen! I followed him up to the solar, a room that I love because it reminds me of my own parents' manor at Combe. It is hung with tapestries just like those my mother and sisters make with their long fingers. And I love it because that's where Isobel sits, my fiery young cousin with a head full of stories – just like me. When Sir John showed me a letter, hung with a heavy wax seal imprinted with the shape of a lion, I noticed her eyes were shining with excitement.

"This is Piers De Montald's seal, William," he explained. "It is by his grace that I hold the manor of Walton and the land around. He has not called upon me in a while, knowing of my arm wound. But now he is holding a tournament at Barham Castle and wants me to compete on his behalf."

"You mean you will joust, like a true knight?" I asked excitedly. "Yes, I hope, like a true knight!" Sir John laughed."You shall accompany me as my squire and we shall take Adam, too. He is already preparing."

Lady Eva looked stricken and quietly left the room. I don't think Sir John noticed. He clapped me on the back happily; then his steward called him away to deal with household matters. "This knight's days seem filled with household accounts," he grumbled as he left.

Isobel looked delighted. "Oh William, isn't it

exciting? Now you are my father's squire you shall carry his lances and shield to the joust. It will be like one of the knightly stories!"

"Now I know why your eyes are so bright," I replied. "I believe you love knights in stories more than anything in the world. Your head is filled with them – good ones, bad ones, red ones, white ones..."

"And your head is stuffed with broken quills," she snapped back, annoyed by my teasing. "The truest bravest knights are all in stories."

I was stung by what she said. I want to think that I am brave and true. An idea popped into my head and then straight out of my mouth because I thought it would impress her: "That's wrong, and I can prove it. I am going to find a true knight."

"How will you do that?" Isobel gasped, her eyes widening. I was pleased by the effect I was having on her, so I carried on. "Well, I shall start by discovering what a true knight is, and then I shall know where to look," I blabbed.

"Oh that's easy. In stories a true knight is brave and loyal, chivalrous, gentle and gracious, good at rescuing those weaker than himself... and he is a champion at whatever he tries. Do you think there is such a man in real life?" Isobel asked eagerly.

"Yes, and I shall find him," I boasted.

"He will be your quest! Then, when you become a knight, you can be like him," Isobel cried. "You must write down everything you discover and read me the story of your success on your return!" she declared.

"If my lady wishes it, I shall do it," I spouted and bowed with a suitable flourish.

Well, that's that. I must pack my parchment scraps and the ink I have begged and borrowed, and take them with me on my journey to Barham. Isobel has even written my quest out grandly and made me sign it. I can't get out of it now even if I wanted to.

The Quest of William De Combe

What makes a true knight and does one exist in the world?

I declare that my quest is to find such a man and return with my tale to the fair Lady Isobel De Walton.

I shall write a diary containing what I discover so that when the time comes I, William De Combe, will be ready to become a true knight myself.

This I swear.

William De Combe,
squire to Sir John De Walton

Year of Our Lord 1332

9 June 1332

It's raining outside, which has put paid to my uncle practising his jousting skills. Instead Adam and I have been burnishing his armour by stirring it in a barrelful of sand and vinegar.

As he poked at the armour I asked Adam why he thought that Lady Eva had seemed so upset about the joust.

"She is used to running the estate while uncle is away, is she not?" I asked.

"Oh yes, and very well she does it, too. But Sir John is in his thirty-fourth year now. At his age, bones creak, and accidents sometimes befall at tournaments – though pray God not to your uncle," he muttered.

"You mean a lance blow or a fall?" I asked.

"Most likely a fall, and then being dragged along by a galloping horse," Adam explained. "That's how knights usually die jousting. That's most likely what's bothering your aunt."

"But surely, isn't it the duty of a true knight to fight or to joust for his lord? She must know that," I asked.

"Of course, but women are soft creatures, William. Didn't you know?" He grinned. I said nothing but I think that he is wrong for once. I do not believe my aunt is soft; I think she has a strong heart.

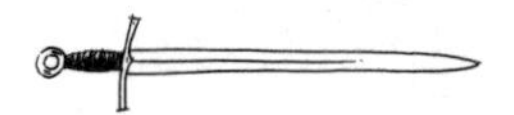

10 June 1332

When I was first sent to Walton, in my eleventh year, I learnt to be a page. I carved the meat for my uncle and aunt and served them at supper. I learnt Latin from the chaplain (and was often beaten for my slowness. Though I knew English well enough from my mother's teaching, he said that wouldn't do for a nobleman.) I learnt to hunt and to shoot an arrow straight, and to serve my aunt however I could. But now I am a squire my life has changed, and when I become a knight it will change again, no doubt. As it is now I must serve my uncle above all, and learn what I can from him.

Today he practised jousting down by the fruit orchard, with me as his assistant. We started at the quintain post. I set up its swinging arm with the shield on one side and the heavy sack on the other. It trembled as Sir John thundered forward on Bayard, tilted his lance and hit the shield full-square in the centre. (He always does. If he didn't he would get clouted by the sack and I've never seen that happen yet.)

Afterwards he galloped towards the wooden rings I had hung up on the branches of the apple trees, and slipped them, one by one, on to his lance.

"Hah!" he growled triumphantly and wheeled round. "Set the rings up again, William!" he shouted, fired up and looking magnificent on his warhorse. He lifted his lance and shook it victoriously.

"We leave for Barham Castle in ten days' time. Sir John is a happy man and all bodes well!" I told Bayard as I walked him back to the stables. But I spoke too quickly. After practice my uncle developed a raging toothache. He is bellowing once again. I am keeping well out of the way, in the stables with my quill.

20 June 1332

"I wish you had more help on this journey, William," Lady Eva told me this morning. She had come out to find me as I was preparing the packhorses for our trip. I smiled at her to show that she should not worry, and showed her how safely we had packed Sir John's tournament clothes and helmet plumes. She tried to sound cheerful. "I believe you are to ride to Copthorne Priory today. Won't you find your younger brother Matthew there? He is learning to be a monk, isn't he?"

"Yes, I can't wait to see him!" I replied, delighted to be reminded. Then I felt guilty and blushed because I felt so excited to be leaving Walton, and my aunt was so cast down by it.

Isobel came out and made me blush once again by handing me an embroidered cap she had made herself. "Go forth, knights of the round table," she cried. "Bring me back a unicorn!"

Sir John laughed and called her a "mad maid full of tall tales." He parted from my aunt with a gentle kiss and a whispered farewell, then he mounted his horse and gave a loud hunting cry: "Halloo!"

We were a small party. Sir John was upon a black riding horse, leading Bayard by the reins so as not to tire him out before the tournament.

I was on a grey mount carrying the tournament shield and lances as best I could, and Adam rode behind leading the packhorses loaded with jousting equipment. We rode out of the manor gates and on through the village. The villagers who were not working in the fields came out to wish us well.

"Godspeed."

"God go with you, Sir John."

They are my uncle's people. They owe everything they have to his favour, just as he owes all he has to Piers De Montald.

So the world works.

We are to ride for several days, further than I have ever been. Which way my path lies I cannot tell, and must trust to God.

We have had a good hour or two's riding and now we have stopped to give the horses a drink.

"We will easily reach the Priory of Copthorne by nightfall. We can afford a rest," Sir John explained. "Now, William. You may fish out your writing things and scribble for a while. I know

Kitchen
Well
Gatehouse

Great Hall
Solar – lord's private rooms
Stables
Moat
The Manor of Walton
Year of our Lord 1332

you will be itching to do so, and Isobel has told me I must let you chronicle our journey every day without teasing you about your obsession with ink. I dare not argue with her and nor should you. Let's hope we live up to her idea of knights on a brave adventure."

It was then that I decided to speak about my quest, hoping he wouldn't laugh at me. "I will certainly chronicle our journey for Lady Isobel, but I have another reason for writing, a sort of quest. I hope to find out what makes a true knight, and record it in words," I ventured.

Sir John looked amazed, and Adam stared too. "Well then, you shall be a busy squire… We shall try to help you, shan't we, Adam?" my uncle said at last. He was grinning more than I'd like so I didn't mention the fact that I was actually looking for a flesh-and-blood true knight. I am afraid he would think me crazy. I wondered to myself whether he had ever met one, but didn't dare ask.

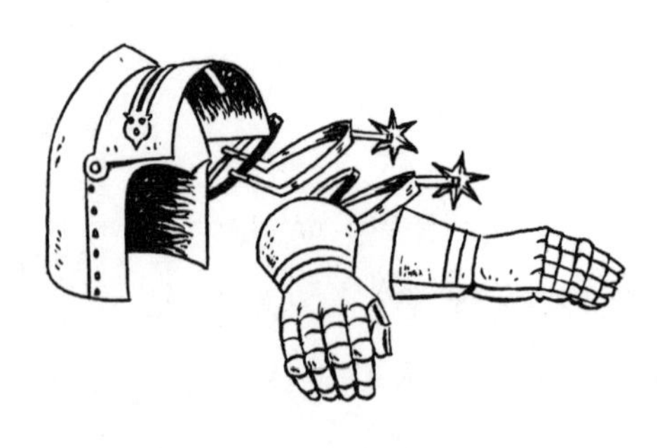

20 June 1332

Evening, the Priory of Copthorne

If I were a monk at Copthorne Priory I would have to sleep in a hard bed and have to get up again for night-time prayers almost as soon as my eyes were closed. I would have to obey the prior in all things, live in this priory forever, and give away all my possessions. Thank the Lord I was the older brother, so it was my young brother Matthew, not me, who was sent to be a monk. I have landed in more luxury, in the priory guest house with Sir John.

Matthew has grown, and at fourteen he almost has the face of a man. He no longer rides or chases or climbs trees, as we used to do back home. Instead his days are measured by learning and by sessions of prayer day and night. I asked him what he prayed for.

"For you, of course, William," he told me. "And for the family and King Edward and all the lords and ladies who have given riches to the priory. Tonight I will pray for our uncle's toothache and for his safety at the joust." And he gave me a sweet smile. He is still a good-looking boy, more handsome than me, though as a monk he will never have a wife.

Matthew took me to the scriptorium where he is learning to write beautifully, by copying the holy texts. He embellishes his work with red ink as well as black, and sometimes even costly blue ink made from a precious stone.

"Do you still write?" he asked me, and when I told him that I did, he grinned.

"I knew you would, William. It is inside you, just as it is in me. I've spoken all about you to the holy brothers who teach me and they have allowed me to save some scraps for you."

He handed me some pieces of parchment which are better quality than I have ever had before, because the monks have made them, scraping and stretching the best goatskin. He also gave me three new quills and a small pot of ink. He made it himself from oak galls steeped in water and mixed with all manner of ingredients which make a fearful poison as well as a good ink. I have wrapped it inside some cloth to keep it safe. I was embarrassed as I had nothing to give him back, but he laughed when I told him I was sorry.

"What do I need, William? I am fed and looked after here in the priory in return for my prayers. I don't need weapons and fine clothes like you." He is happy, I think, so I am happy for him. My candle is burning lower. I must hurry up and tell the whole story of this day before I sleep.

Sir John's toothache was raging by the time we reached the priory. It did nothing for his temper. Just before we reached the gates it began to rain, and he swore so loudly and roundly that two monks working in a nearby field stood up and crossed themselves.

Adam told me in a whisper why he thought

my uncle's bad temper was not simply caused by his tooth. "Sir John does not care much for the prior in charge of this place and you shall see why," he winked. "This toothache will keep him here a day longer than he likes."

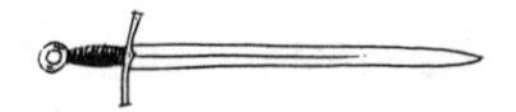

The prior welcomed us at the gate. He is a thin tall man, with cheekbones like knives and a pointed face. When he heard about uncle's toothache he took him straight to the infirmary (thankfully empty of sick monks).

"Sir John De Walton is our honoured guest. He has the toothache," the prior announced to a small nervously-thin monk who glanced anxiously at his grand new patient. He was used to treating his own priory brothers I could see, but not knights with an uncertain temper. The monk bowed and motioned to Sir John to sit on a bed, then shuffled out and returned with a pot of some unknown mixture.

"This ointment will dull the pain somewhat if you rub it in. It is my own mix of vinegar, oil and sulphur, but it will not cure the problem completely. You must have this tooth pulled to rid yourself of the poisonous worms that live inside it. With your gracious assent I will do it tomorrow."

At that the prior looked rather gleeful, I thought. My uncle went a little pale. "Harrumph," he exclaimed and stood up, glaring at the monks. Then he stalked off back to the guest house.

Later he was invited to dine in the prior's private quarters with me in attendance, and I found out why he was so wary of his host. Beforehand, Adam warned me: "Say nothing tonight, William. And be prepared for trouble!"

The evening began well enough, with roast meat, then sweet honeyed fruits (unwise for a toothache, I thought). The prior had wine brought from his cellar, and Sir John said it was fine. But the conversation did not flow well and eventually the prior began to attack my uncle with his words.

"Tournaments are a sin. It is a sin to fight for sport when you should be fighting for God in the Holy Land," he insisted, stabbing the air with his finger. I knew my uncle was irritated because he banged down his goblet in reply.

"My good prior. I see no harm in sport. And as for going on crusade, we have trouble enough to deal with on England's borders. The Scots and the French would love to see our best fighting forces disappear off to Jerusalem." The prior's eyes blazed at that.

"The Pope pronounces that jousting is a sin, and that Jerusalem should be reclaimed for Christianity. It is the duty of every true knight of this realm to fight for God and not for a purse of money in a tournament!" he snapped.

Sir John finally exploded with a bull roar. "Good Heavens, man! If we don't defend you

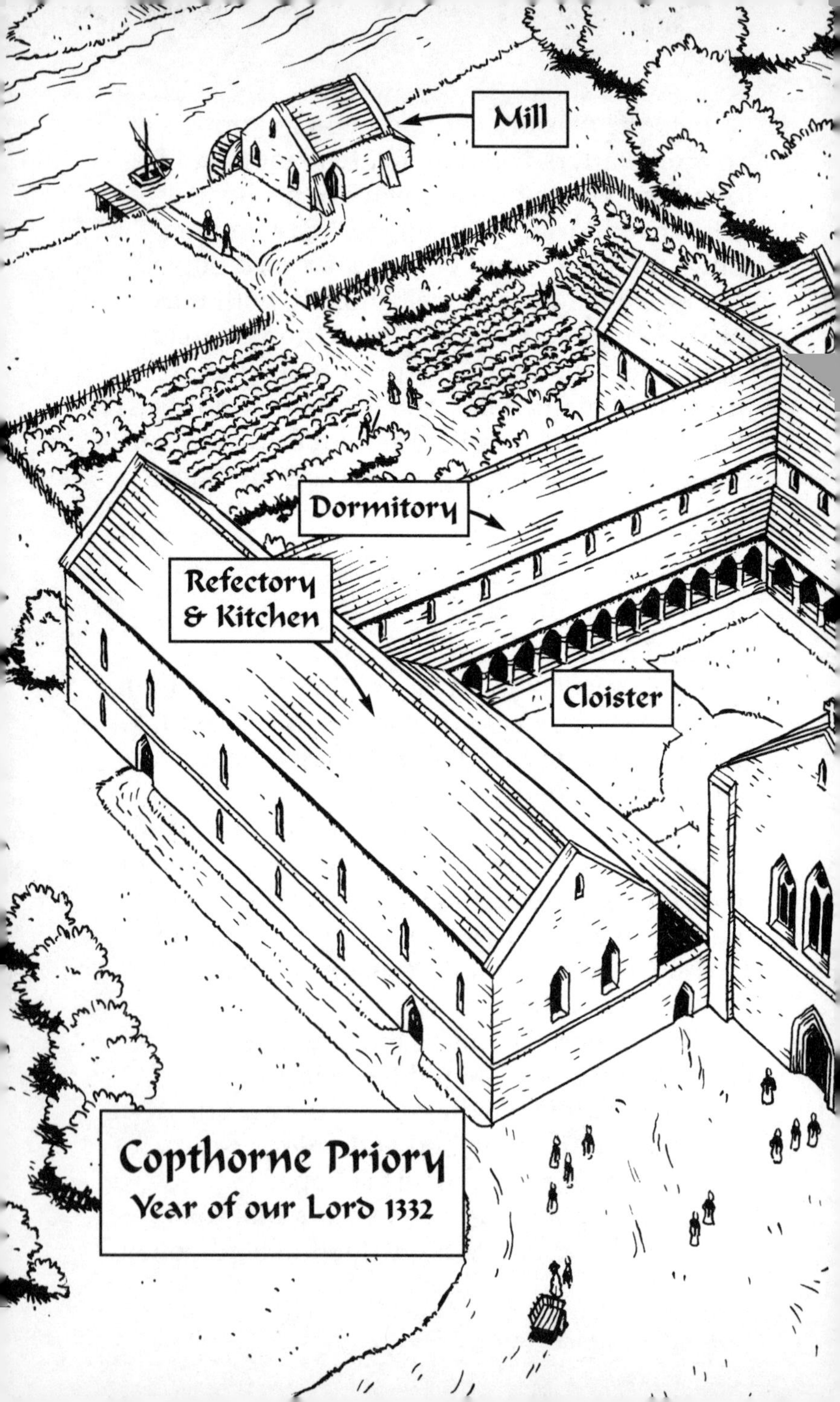
Mill
Dormitory
Refectory & Kitchen
Cloister
Copthorne Priory
Year of our Lord 1332

Church
Dormitory

from the Scots and the French you shall one day find yourself dead in a ditch! Argh!" He winced at the pain of his tooth and clutched at his cheek.

"Pain is a mark of sin," the prior announced loftily, looking self-satisfied and not in the least sympathetic to my uncle's pain.

My uncle stood up abruptly. "I should go. You have prayers, do you not?" he growled.

"I shall pray for your soul, and for the return of Jerusalem to the Christian fold," the prior replied, and pointedly bit into a sugared fruit.

After that dinner my uncle was in no mood for company, so I found Adam at the stables. He was not surprised when I told him about the disastrous argument at dinner. "The prior longs for the past, when knights marched off to the Holy Land in the name of God. But things are different now. Sir John won't ever be going on a crusade. Never was and never will."

I thought long about this. Since I was a small child I remember sitting by the flickering fire, seeing pictures in the flames, as my mother told me tales of crusading heroes. She told me how her own grandfather had ridden away on a holy mission to recapture Jerusalem. If the prior was right, that holy crusading knights were the only true knights, then my quest was doomed to failure, for I would never find one. Adam told the story of a true knight differently. "Nowadays most people think it is a knight's first duty to protect his own people and country," he said. So it seems a true knight need not go away to Jerusalem these days, and my quest is still possible.

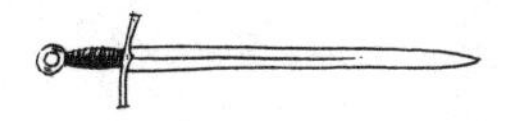

21 June 1332

Sir John had his tooth pulled and to my relief he made hardly any noise about it, even though the monk used fearsome iron tools that looked as if they came from a blacksmith's workshop. My uncle was given something, a syrup of some kind, by the monk, who said it contained a plant called henbane mixed with a strong drink. It seemed to quieten him and though we stood by, we didn't need to hold him down. My uncle may not be very holy, but there is no doubt that today he was brave. He has rested since the tooth came out, and I have been able to explore the priory with Matthew.

22 JUNE 1332

"You should stay, Sir John. The sky looks set for midsummer rain," the prior advised us as we saddled up ready to leave this morning. But, despite his pain being gone, my uncle was not in the mood to hear any more lectures. "It's no matter to us," he replied shortly. "Give us your blessing, Prior. We must set off now to reach the town of Totbury by evening time."

The prior, sensibly, decided not to argue. But he was right about the weather. The air seemed sticky and thick, and a while after we left rain began to patter on the ground. It swiftly became more heavy and ran down our cheeks in rivulets as we rode. My uncle and Adam bowed their heads, urging the horses forward every now and again.

"Come on, boy." "Easy, lad." Suddenly there was a flash and a thunderbolt shot from the heavens, followed by a roar like a dragon's cry. Adam struggled to keep the packhorses in line. "Whoa there!"

"This storm will please the prior," my uncle

growled. "He would no doubt tell us that God sends thunder and lightning to punish sins." Then he turned aside on to a smaller track beneath an arch of trees that gave us protection from the lashing rain. "We will have to take shelter at this rate. There was a village through these woods when I was a boy. Follow me."

The woodland thickened, and the track uncle had chosen almost disappeared under thick brambles. We had to mind out for twisted roots that snaked out unseen from the trees. The packhorses shied several times and even Bayard seemed uncertain.

"Such dark old woods can spook horses," Adam explained.

"I have heard there is old evil lurking in such places," I muttered nervously.

"Murderous Scots hide in woods like these up north," my uncle remarked. "Those devils would love to set up an ambush on such a gloomy path."

"Are there any wolves hereabouts?" I asked, mindful of old tales I had heard tell of fierce packs of wolves intent on a human meal. Uncle didn't say no. Instead he made me feel worse.

"Let's hope the Coterels aren't waiting for us in some shadows, eh?" he whispered, looking sideways at me.

"The what?" I replied.

My uncle sucked his breath in through his

teeth. "Don't you know? The Coterels are a band of lawless brothers, knights gone to the bad, a rabble of thieves that kidnap to make their living," he explained. I must have looked terrified because he began to laugh and leant out of his saddle to clap me on the back.

"Don't worry, boy. There are no Coterels in these parts, and no wolves either. Those were all hunted down by my grandfather. As for evil spirits lurking in the woods, say your prayers and you should be safe."

The wood thinned, the track widened, and my hopes rose that we would soon be sitting by a kind villager's cooking fire. But instead we found a village that was sadly broken down. There were a few scattered houses but they were deserted, some with their thatched roofs caved in. Where once there were strips of field filled with crops for each household there were now just choking seas of weed.

"It was an old village, once called Finholt," my uncle explained. "We can tether the horses and shelter in the best hovel for the night."

Inside the hovel's one dirt-floored room we were dry enough.

"Where are the people of this village?" I asked, puzzled and not a little scared.

Sir John sat forward and looked serious: "It was God's will to bring us a terrible famine, just before you were born. The harvest failed for two years in a row and the people hereabouts could not feed themselves or their cattle. I remember them coming to Walton to beseech us for help, their bones showing as if death had already stripped them of flesh. We were their lords and so it was our duty to help them, but it was hard for all, even at Walton. We had little enough food for ourselves."

"Did the people die?" I whispered.

"Some... The old and the very young. Others left to try their luck begging in the towns."

My uncle sighed. He looked quite stricken. Adam turned away from my gaze too. He must have suffered the famine as well, though he had never spoken of it. My uncle stood up and shook his boots as if to throw the memories off.

"I hope your writing tools aren't damp, boy. You'd better be mindful of Isobel and write your piece for the day. And don't forget to mention the bloodthirsty Coterels. She'll love that!" he added. "And I think you have learnt something for your quest today – that a knight, however true, cannot conjure up a crop to save his people, but he must try his best to feed them, William. He must try his best."

Now I am writing by the failing light outside. I don't see how I shall sleep tonight, as lightning and thunder play so loudly outside. To make it worse, every time I hear the horses nearby whinnying or blowing through their nostrils, I jump, thinking of wolves and wood spirits. I had best say my prayers, as my uncle advises.

23 June 1332
Totbury

It must be nearly midnight but there are still plenty of noisy merrymakers outside on the streets of Totbury, so I am writing instead of sleeping. I am in an upstairs corner of an ale house, sitting by a window to get some air (this place smells horribly of stale beer). Sir John has the best room in the place but even that has only a rickety bed small enough for a child. When I looked in on him just now he had given up on the bed and was asleep in a high-backed chair. Adam is staying with the horses to keep them safe; he's probably more comfortable than we are. Since I cannot sleep I will write down the day's events by the light of a candle I have found half-burnt in a bowl.

By the time we arrived in Totbury this afternoon a midsummer bonfire was already flaming in one of its meadows, even though the sky was still full of summer light. People were running towards the field, crying out to their friends, and carrying lighted torches. Those torches seemed to wave dangerously near the higgledy-piggledy wooden buildings overhanging the narrow lanes of the town. I felt scared to see so many houses all crowded together, at least thirty I think.

"You can tell it's the eve of Saint John the Baptist's Day. I reckon this lot have been celebrating with their ale pots since dawn," Adam remarked, as a ragged party of townspeople sang and danced their way past us. "Mind your head," he added, and I ducked just in time to avoid the iron ale house sign that jutted out into the lane. The landlord's boy took our horses for stabling and the landlord himself grunted at us and thumped down pots of ale and some rabbit stew. To my mind he did not show Sir John enough respect.

"Don't you think he's rude?" I whispered to Adam once we were seated. My uncle overheard me.

"You have not travelled far in the world, William. When you do, you will find that the people alter as much as the land. The landlord would not dare to be rude to me; it's just that his manners are not those of my own villeins."

I thought to myself that now I have gone so far from home I seem to have changed, too, and feel

like a small child again in an unknown world.

"Eat up, lads. Let's go and see the fun in the midsummer field," my uncle smiled.

Later on, we walked towards the meadow where the bonfire was burning, and as I tagged along behind I suddenly heard a strange noise – a "snrgg, snarg, snuffle" sort of noise. A beast's shadow fell onto the wall beside me, and I froze, terrified.

Then, to my deep embarrassment, a small pig trotted out of an alleyway, looked at me balefully and then went on her way. I breathed again, then wished I hadn't because I had stepped into a pile of her foul smelly mess on the road.

"No wonder this town stinks. They leave their animals to wander freely and throw their rubbish in the street," I muttered angrily. Suddenly I realised I had lost sight of Adam and my uncle. The only thing I could do was to follow the crowd and hope that I spotted them.

There was quite a party going on in the field. People milled between the stalls and the shows and there were plenty of ways to spend money.

"Throw the dice and win a prize."

"See the juggler throw six balls!"

"Try your luck at bowling... skittles... throwing the hammer..."

A pedlar caught my eye. "Ribbons! Ribbons for your lady!" he cried, a wooden box full of wares hanging round his neck. I bought a comb for Isobel. "May your lady be fair," the pedlar said, giving me a toothless grin.

Then I noticed a crowd gathered in one corner of the field. Some of them were shouting: "Come on, miller! Come on!" I pushed my way through to look for Sir John, and saw a huge man wrestling a much smaller one to the ground.

"No one can beat the miller," someone cried, as the smaller man crawled off, defeated and bruised. I turned and bumped straight into a friar in a long grubby gown. He was looking eagerly at me.

"I'll give you a lucky saint's relic if you fight the miller," he said. I stared at him, astonished. His pudgy face screwed up into a sort of smile. "I have sacred relics of the saints here in my possession. I'll give you one of my most precious, Saint Apolonia's fingerbone, if you beat the miller at wrestling. It will cure all sorts of illness and bring you good luck." He pulled out a small bone from a leather pouch and cradled it in his palm as if it were made of gold. I stared and wondered for a moment whether I should buy the bone, never for once thinking about trying to wrestle the miller. A holy relic would surely bring luck and help Sir John in the joust.

Seeing my hesitation the friar pressed it into my hand and to my horror he cried out loudly.

"This boy has agreed to fight! Look at him! He'll be a nimble and clever wrestler. Worth a wager, I'd say." The crowd turned towards me and before I knew it they were lifting me into the centre of the circle where the miller stood, as wide as a stable door with a head the size of a bucket.

"Throw him!" someone shouted.

"Come on! Get in there!" the crowd grew louder. "I'll wager on the miller!" I heard the friar's voice ring out clearly above the rest. The traitor was betting against me. I think he had one or two takers too.

I stood frozen on the spot as if enchanted, clutching the bone in my hand. The miller strode over and grabbed me. His big hands closed over my arms and he lifted me up like a baby, growling horribly all the while. But then, suddenly, a cry went up: "Fire! There's fire down at the baker's house!" The miller looked startled and let go of me.

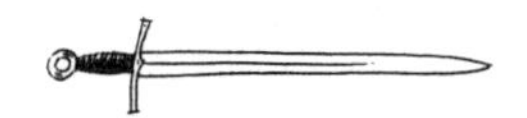

"Quickly! Get the buckets! Pull up water from the well!" people shouted. The crowd melted away, running down the field back to the town to save the baker's shop – and perhaps the rest of the town from burning.

The friar remained, looking disappointed that I had not been pulverised by the miller. He made as if to snatch the saint's bone from my hand.

"Leave my squire alone," Sir John's voice boomed out. To my great relief Adam and my uncle appeared at my side. The friar looked from one to the other. "I must go and help quench the fire," he muttered and ran away.

"We should help, too," I blurted out. "There's a fire in the town!"

"What fire?" Sir John whispered. "Oh, you mean the fire I made up and shouted about to save you from a pasting? Come on, boy. This midsummer party is going to go on all night, but I think you need to stay out of trouble. We'll go back to the ale house and you can return to your ink and paper world for a while. Write about how true knights always do their best to save people in distress! Oh, and I'd throw away that old pig's bone if I were you."

I have never felt so foolish or so grateful for the guidance of my uncle. The world outside Walton seems a place of baffling surprises.

24 JUNE 1332

It is the next morning, yet I have had little sleep. The revellers are still outside, alternately singing and tumbling drunkenly into the ditches, by the sound of it. Last night the ale house was crowded and we were all pressed together drinking the landlord's weak, watery beer.

A man in a brightly coloured coat raised his pot to me in a friendly way. "Are you on your way to the joust at Barham?" he asked. "I saw your horses in the stable. I am going there, too, to make a purse of money, I hope."

"How will you do that?" I asked in surprise, and to my amazement he drained his pot, jumped up on to one of the wooden tables, took out some wooden balls and began to juggle them. Others gathered round, clapped and laid coins on the table, and someone struck up a tune on a pipe.

"Tell us a story, Tom!" someone cried out, and the juggler hopped down off the table.

"I shall tell a story for a penny, about a gentle knight and his lady," he announced. Sir John

stood up and flipped him a coin. "Tell my squire here. He likes to collect stories, but I am going to my bed. Don't be long, William. I will leave Adam here to stop you from wrestling."

The juggler sat down beside me and Adam, though others were listening. "Well then. This gentle knight was called Sir Tristrem. He rode over hill and dale to find a true lady..." he began, but then another voice broke in.

"What rubbish. A knight only rides hill and dale to find a fortune for himself!" I saw that the voice belonged to the friar who had so nearly got me into trouble wrestling the miller.

"Watch out for trouble. I reckon that friar has drunk more ale than the rest of us," Adam murmured.

The storyteller frowned at the interruption but carried on. "Sir Tristrem was gentle and full of grace–"

"Not any knight I know of," the friar heckled, and this time some of the crowd laughed. But again the storyteller ignored it.

"Whenever he could he used his shining sword to save the poor and the defenceless from harm," he continued.

"This man wasn't a knight at all!" the friar cried. "Knights only fight for booty. They take what they like from the poor; the more defenceless the victim, the more they take."

I heard one or two onlookers draw in their breath at this. "And friars are not all holy and good," someone shouted out. It was clear the friar had gone too far. The irritated storyteller spat on the floor and gave up on the story of Sir Tristrem.

"Let's check the horses," Adam said quietly, and pulled me away from the crowd. Out in the stables it was much quieter and we could talk. I was very troubled by the friar's words.

I asked Adam, "Do some knights fight only for money, for booty they can steal?"

Adam looked me in the eye. "Armies take what they like from the lands of their enemies, and what they don't take they often destroy. Many a town has been sacked by knights who are busy killing the locals while their squires load the horses up with all the goods they can carry away," he said.

"So the friar was right. Knights are not gentle, or full of grace. Those knights are only in stories!" I cried. Adam shrugged.

"Then a true knight does not really exist!" I blurted out, and to my horror I felt tears stinging in my eyes. I turned away so that Adam wouldn't see them fall.

25 June 1332

We have been riding all morning and now we have reached a ridge from where we can look across a valley towards a magnificent castle standing on a hill. A road snakes over the valley floor, sprinkled with groups of men and horses moving towards the castle as if it were pulling them by magic.

When I saw the place I gasped at its size.

"That is Barham," my uncle explained. "When we get there keep your eyes and ears open, boy. You will find a great deal to scribble about, I promise. But first let's rest the horses and ourselves."

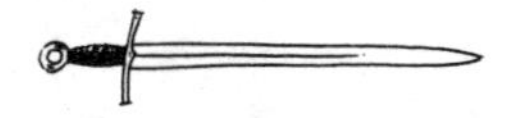

As soon as we dismounted I burrowed into my saddlebag and found my writing equipment. I feel as if a dam of words is bursting inside me, probably because yesterday I felt too melancholy to write much.

We were still in Totbury yesterday. I spent much of the time skulking around in the shadows near the blacksmith's workshop, where we had a repair done on Sir John's jousting helm. I felt sleepy and I thought the loud banging of the blacksmith's tools would keep me from dozing, but it didn't. Eventually Adam woke me by tickling my nose with a bird's feather.

"Hey, slug-a-bed, I've found a quill for you," he said. Later I got my parchment and my ink ready but I found I didn't know what to write. I certainly had no romantic knightly tales to tell Isobel, though I imagine that she will laugh at the pig and the wrestling match. As for my quest to find a true knight, I was thinking of giving it up since I heard that instead of shining heroes, many knights were just thieving murderers.

I felt just as miserable this morning, even though I knew we would be on our way. "You look fed up, boy. Aren't you looking forward to reaching Barham Castle?" Sir John remarked when he saw me.

"I am feeling downcast," I admitted.

"Then we shall talk about it as we ride. Are the packhorses ready, Adam? Good. Then say goodbye to Totbury!" my uncle cried. We rode out of the town and he pulled his horse alongside mine. "Now tell me why you are so glum, William. Are you sick?" he asked.

"No Sire," I replied, and decided to explain how I felt. "It's about my quest," I began.

"Oh yes. You are hoping to discover what makes a true knight," Uncle murmured.

"Well, yes..." I replied, still preferring not to tell him I am actually looking for a real one.

"And what have you found so far?" he asked.

"I have found that true knights should fight for their lord, and they should try to look after the people on their estates, and they should be brave and some of them fight for God..." I said, feeling awkward and glancing at him. "If I am to be a knight one day I must know all this, but..." I hesitated.

"Yes?" Uncle replied expectantly, so I plunged on, nervously gabbling out what I had to say: "I have been told that many knights kill ordinary people so they can steal possessions and land, and now I am fearful that a true knight, that is one who is as good as a story knight, may not exist in the world at all!"

I feared my uncle might be angry that I was so outspoken, but instead he replied calmly: "When your father sent you to be my squire he expected me to teach you all there is to know about being a knight, William. I shall try my best, and I won't lie, so listen well. It is true that when armies of knights go to fight on enemy territory they lay waste enemy lands and gather booty from its villages and towns, and, yes, they may kill any people that they find. It is certainly one of the ways that real knights differ from those in stories."

He put his hand on my shoulder. "The truth is that, good or bad, in battle a knight must fight and kill to survive," he explained. "You know that, William. You have trained with your weapons ready to do so yourself. Now, if knights take their killing ways to the enemy towns and villages, and load their squires up with stolen goods, well, it is all part of defeating the enemy." He looked at me to satisfy himself that I understood. Then he smiled and spurred onwards.

As we rode on I thought about what I had heard, both at Totbury and Copthorne, and I came to realise that if I am to continue my quest my idea of a true knight must change, and I must explain it as best I can to Isobel when I return to her. What is a true knight after all? Surely it must be someone who lives, not some impossible character made only of words. The true knight I seek must be someone who rides in the world as it really is, bad as well as good.

Once I had worked this out in my mind I had an important question to ask my uncle, so I spurred my horse to catch up with him on the track. "Tell me what it is like to fight in battle," I said. "What is it truly like?"

"I think we had better stop for that one," Uncle replied and reined in his horse. Adam led the horses to a stream to drink, while my uncle purposefully gathered up a handful of stones and then sat on the ground with me.

"Imagine that you are standing with thousands of men – archers, knights and the men-at-arms the knights have brought with them from home. This line here is your army." He laid out a line of stones on the ground.

"You can see the enemy in the distance. There they are, over there." He laid out another line of stones facing the first. "You've got your orders from your commanders so you know where to stand, and you are waiting for the action to start," he added. (Probably trying to swallow down my fear, I thought silently.)

My uncle scattered some more stones behind the army lines: "Your squires and servants, like Adam here, would be back behind the army looking after your equipment and horses. You'll need them later."

"How close would we be to the enemy?" I asked, trying to picture the scene.

"Just close enough to hear their shouts on a breeze," Uncle replied. "There may be other things between you and them – ditches to trip up enemy horses and lines of stakes to delay them getting through... Ideally your leaders will have chosen the battlefield site and snatched the best position for your army."

I tried to imagine the sounds: the noise of one's own breathing inside a stifling helmet, enemy shouts getting closer...

"Will the enemy charge us first?" I asked.

"Maybe. If your commanders think you can withstand the enemy's charges again and again until they weaken, then that's the tactic they use. Don't forget, as an Englishman you have the world's best archers on your side. They will start by firing hundreds of arrows towards the enemy."

My imaginary picture darkened as its sky filled with a curtain of arrows whistling across the space between the armies. The command rings out: "Fire!" One volley arches overhead, then another, and another.

"Saint George! Saint George!" Uncle gave a battlecry to start an English charge, and he pushed the lines of stones together on the ground. "Now sword meets sword and the best fighters win, or the biggest army," he said. "The armies will regroup now and again, but only to begin another charge, not to rest. It can go on for hours."

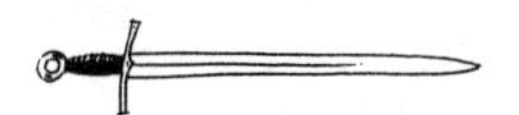

He sat back on his heels, throwing a few stones away into the bushes. "Some men will die. Some will be injured, and some may turn tail and run if they are on the losing side. The victors will mount their warhorses and ride after men to finish them off. That's when knights look to capture some valuable prisoners." He opened the palm of one hand and showed me one large stone he had saved: "Here is a noble-born prisoner – your profit from the battle. Later you'll be able to get a fat ransom from his family to set him free."

"But what is it really like to fight?" I pressed. I could picture the scene, but I was struggling to grasp how it actually felt to look through the slit of a helmet and fight for your life. Sir John thought for a minute. Then he pulled his sword out from its scabbard on his belt and he slashed it towards an imaginary enemy. "It's noisy, bloody and hot," he said baldly and sheathed his sword with a finality that showed our conversation was over.

Yet I knew there was more to tell. He had fought the Scots, and had the scars to show for it, but the dying screams of men and horses, the smells of fear… it seems my uncle prefers to keep them to himself. Maybe they are things that cannot be described, and perhaps it is best that I do not know of them. But I sensed there must also be some other feeling, something exciting and powerful, that comes to a knight in battle. For why else would my uncle love it so?

After he had put away his sword he stood up and patted Bayard's flank. The huge horse nuzzled his head into his master's arm. "We shall charge again soon, my old friend," my uncle murmured to him. "Saint George! Saint George! We shall taste victory once more."

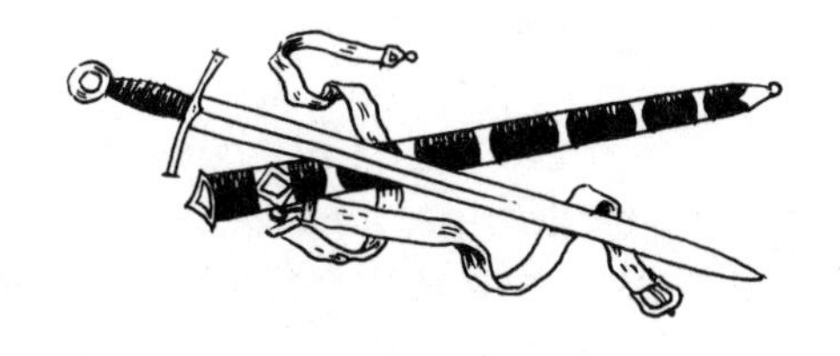

26 June 1332

I have entered another world, a castle world: of feasts and flags; where there are more rooms, stairs and servants than I ever dreamt of. Barham has great towers and walls surrounding it and inside it is many times bigger than the manor at Walton.

As we rode towards it we saw Piers De Montald's men patrolling the walkways along the top of the walls, all wearing the blue and gold livery of their master. When we reached the guards at the castle drawbridge I saw close up that the gold on their tabards was embroidery in the shape of a lion.

Inside the walls there was a big courtyard surrounded by buildings, and to me it seemed as busy and as noisy as Totbury. Servants were rushing to and fro across the worn grass. Hunting dogs barked in their kennels, horses whinnied and guards shouted orders. Someone was digging furiously in a kitchen garden, while someone else clanked a bucket as they drew water from a well.

"Adam, see our horses are stabled, and our tent is put up in the jousting meadow," Sir John said, and he turned away from him. I didn't know what I should be doing.

"Adam, shall I come with you?" I asked, confused. Adam looked surprised.

"Of course not. You are of noble birth. You must go with Sir John," he exclaimed. "I'll see you later."

Sir John looked round and beckoned me. "Are you ready to meet Piers De Montald?" he asked. I had the feeling I was about to step over an edge towards something I didn't know, a place where a person like Adam didn't venture.

"Look lively then, William. We'll be expected in the Great Hall," Sir John ordered, already striding off up the slope towards the keep. It stood squarely ahead of us on its mound, its walls wider, thicker and more impenetrable than those of any other tower I have ever seen. Even though it was still daylight outside, torches burned behind its heavy wooden doors. The air inside smelt of old woodsmoke and the rosemary branches that were scattered among rushes on the floor.

A noise hummed in my ears like a hive of bees and it grew louder as we neared the Great Hall. When we entered the hum exploded into a hubbub of voices. Knights stood with their squires down either side of the hall between its tall stone pillars. We were led to the far end of the hall where a neatly bearded man sat on a carved high-backed chair, one arm resting casually and the other holding a goblet.

"Sir John De Walton, my Lord," a steward announced, and I quickly copied my uncle who bent his knee and bowed his head.

"Sir John! The best jouster in my team! You are most welcome," the man grinned. "How is your arm? Are you sure it is ready for aiming a lance?" he asked.

"As good as new, my Lord," my uncle replied.

On either side of the Lord sat two women: one long-necked elegant lady I took to be his wife and one girl about fourteen, who turned out to be his daughter.

Sir John bowed his head towards the ladies. "Lady Eleanor; Lady Anne. My heart is greatly eased by seeing such beauty," he announced, much to my surprise. Where did he get such a silver tongue? I have never heard him talk that way at Walton! The daughter, Anne, fixed eyes the colour of plums upon me, and her gaze made me feel awkward.

"I wish to present my nephew, William De Combe. He is my squire," Sir John announced, gently pushing me forward.

"You are most welcome, William," the Lord

replied. Up close I could see that his velvet gown was finely embroidered with tiny lions, and I thought that was apt. The smooth way he moved and spoke reminded me of a cat.

"Do you wish to be a knight one day, William?" he asked.

"Oh yes, I wish to be a true knight above all things," I replied.

"Good, good," he purred. "Well, you shall see some of our best knights in action at the tournament, so you may learn from them. Your uncle is one of the very best, of course," he added. My uncle made a tiny bow from his waist. In this grand company he seemed more refined than I had ever seen him before.

Piers De Montald's eyes flicked from me to his dark-eyed daughter. "Lady Anne, take William De Combe on a tour. I wish to speak with Sir John," he said and turned away from me with a brief smile, indicating that our conversation was over. His daughter turned away, too, then glanced back across her shoulder and crooked a finger as an order for me to follow her.

I was too nervous to say anything as we left the Hall and walked along a castle corridor. Eventually she broke the silence.

"There are many squires here with their knights," she remarked. I nodded, tongue-tied. She stopped and look narrowly at me. "You are not gracious, William De Combe. You should have compliments ready. If you want to be a knight you will have to learn to court a lady as well as sword-fighting," she snapped.

"I… I'm sorry. I did not mean to cause offence. I… was made silent by your beauty," I gabbled, trying to copy Sir John's style back in the hall. This seemed to satisfy her, for the moment.

"Do you like poetry, William De Combe?" she remarked as we reached a set of winding stairs.

"Oh yes, I like it very much," I replied, and she looked pleased.

"Then you must write me a poem," she announced. "And then, when you are a knight, I might choose to give you a token of mine to carry, and you will dedicate all your good deeds to me." With that she turned and walked off, abandoning me in a dark castle corner.

My first attempt at knightly chivalry had been an utter disaster.

I wished suddenly and strongly for a taste of home, so I blundered about the castle until I found a way out. Then I searched for Adam. I found him in the jousting meadow by our tent. He had lit a fire to cook himself a soup of onions and beans, and though I am going to a feast tonight I begged him for a morsel. When I told him about Lady Anne his eyebrows went up into his hair.

"I can't help you there, William. I can tell you how to catch a fish or cure a horse of colic, but I've never learnt the ways of chivalry; it's only for knights. You will have to ask your uncle to help you with that sort of thing."

27 June 1332

I am still as full as a pig who has gobbled a pile of acorns. There was so much food at the feast last night I imagined it coming from some magic pot hidden deep in the castle kitchens. The knights, too, looked magical in their finest clothes. The walls of the hall were hung with their banners. Piers De Montald wore an even richer gown than before and his ladies were in gold cloth so finely woven it looked as if it were made of cloud. Minstrels played softly behind them as they sat at the top table along with other important guests, including Sir John. The rest of us sat on long tables stretching down the hall.

I was placed with other squires, who were definitely not magical, just a motley bunch of young squires like me. We ate off slabs of bread as we do at home, but the food was of the best quality. Servant after servant carried in such treats as spinach tartlets, baked eggs, onions and peas, pigs' heads and chickens. There were fishes from the castle moat and plenty of peppery sauces flavoured with exotic spices I could not name. I even saw two servants stagger up to the top table carrying a roasted swan.

ALLEYN'S SCHOOL LIBRARY

After the meats there was spiced wine and we were given sugar-paste lozenges stamped with the shape of a lion. The top table was presented with an entire hunting scene as big as a footstool, all modelled out of sugar paste. I was sitting next to a small knobbly-headed boy who spat on the floor too much for my liking and splashed me when a servant brought round water for hand-washing between courses. After a while he waved his knife towards the top table.

"See that man in red over there? That's Baldwin of Brandenburg, over for the joust. He's won lots of bouts abroad this year. He could give your man Sir John a run for his money."

"I've heard Geoffrey of Ardres is turning up tomorrow," another lad piped up. "He's one of the top jousters in France. Anyways, Sir John is a bit long in the tooth these days."

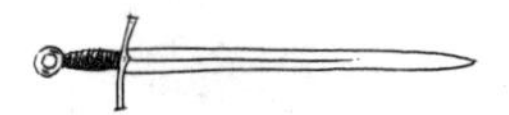

I began to worry for Sir John. It came into my head that I had to tell him these remarks about his rivals straight away. I think my judgement was gone, what with all the wine I had drunk (more than I should have done, because I was feeling nervous). I stood up and made my way towards the top table, trying to sidle round behind it. But before I reached Sir John a small hand shot out and blocked my path. It was the Lady Anne's, and she was looking expectantly at me.

"So, true knight, have you written me a poem

yet?" she asked quite loudly, so that the others around her turned to look at me.

"Er, yes... no!" I gulped. Embarrassed beyond belief, I simply turned round and ran back to my place, only to find that the other squires had watched my failure and were giggling cruelly. Knobbly-head imitated a high-pitched woman's voice: "Oh, what a wonderful thing is love, which makes a man shine with so many virtues! Why, your nose is the shiniest I have ever seen!"

The others joined in: "Look, how pale he is in the presence of his beloved. A sure sign of love, or is it too much ale?" Another idiot remarked, "Why, he is not eating. Pining lovers go off their food, you know."

"Shut up!" I cried. "Ooooh!" they chorused and carried on teasing until I stood up angrily.

At this the other boys guffawed out loud with triumph and the rest of the guests looked round. I sat down again, mortified, and glanced towards the top table, hoping they hadn't seen. No such luck. Anne was looking right at me, while talking to her father, and Sir John had his eye on me too. Then, to my horror, a servant tapped me on the shoulder and told me that Piers De Montald wished to speak with me. I had no choice and had to go back to the top table, with rude comments from the other squires ringing in my ears.

"William, I am told by your uncle that you are

most desirous to discover all the qualities of a true knight," Piers De Montald said. I nodded, at the same time wishing that the ground would swallow me up. "A true knight should know the rules of courtly love," he continued. "He should devote himself to a pure and noble lady and through doing so he will make himself virtuous." Out of the corner of my eye I saw Anne looking self-satisfied.

"Now watch, William, and learn," her father said. He stood up, took his wife's hand and led her to the centre of the room. I thought they were going to dance; but immediately Baldwin of Brandenburg came across and knelt before Lady Eleanor, who was holding out a gold-coloured scarf.

"My mother will choose a jousting champion to wear her favour," Anne hissed in my ear, obviously assuming I was ignorant as well as rude.

Then Baldwin made a play for the scarf with a flowery speech to Lady Eleanor: "God be praised for granting me the chance to see with my own eyes such a treasure, such a pure pearl. My tongue does not have the words to tell of your beauty. I dedicate to you all the deeds that I may do in the joust. I devote myself to your service."

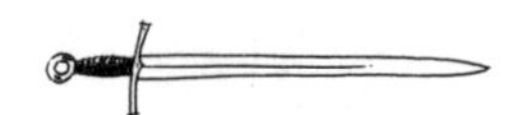

Lady Eleanor smiled, but held on to her scarf. "Then I shall give you my approval when you do well," she replied. But she obviously meant that Baldwin wouldn't be her champion. Other knights came up and paid her compliments, but she still held on tightly to that scarf.

Sir John looked at me with twinkling eyes. "So William. I hear you did not aquit yourself well with young Lady Anne," he murmured.

I was outraged at this. "That's not true! She wanted a poem and I didn't know what to say!" I cried.

"Calm down, boy!" Sir John laughed. "She shouldn't have teased you so. But a true knight should have some manners, some honeyed words for noble ladies. You'll learn some by and by. It's all part of being a good knight, especially at a joust when we fight for the ladies' favour." He stood up, made his way towards Lady Eleanor, and spouted such a bundle of fine words my mouth dropped open. She sighed and handed him the scarf, to the cheers of everyone in the hall.

The old devil! She has chosen him as her jousting champion! Where did my grumpy uncle from Walton get to? In this castle I believe he has turned from one man into another.

Later we made our way by lighted torch to our tent. I decided to tell my uncle what I was secretly pondering. "I am beginning to think this courtly love pretending may be the hardest part of being a true knight. For I should never like to fight for Lady Anne's favour, ever. I think she is a shrew," I admitted.

"I never said that being a true knight was easy, did I?" my uncle laughed.

I have learnt something more for my quest today. I do not believe a knight could be chivalrous to every lady there ever was, that's for sure. Once again, I think I must look to real life to find my true knight, and not to stories.

27 June 1332
Midday

Everything is ready. All morning I have been busy preparing Sir John for the first bout of jousting this afternoon and it is nearly time for the competition to begin, but I am taking a moment or two to write since I think it might help my nerves.

The jousting meadows were already busy when we poked our heads outside our tent this morning. There was lots of last-minute hammering on wooden rails and stands for the spectators. Castle servants were throwing buckets of sand and straw on the jousting ground, then pouring water on it to keep down the dust.

I went to fetch some water and got into a queue. That's when I heard a familiar voice behind me, saying: "There's the squire who loves stories. Good luck!" It was the juggler from the inn at Totbury, here as promised to earn some pennies from the crowd. He waved to me as he hurried by.

"Hey, wait. You never finished the tale of Sir Tristrem," I cried out. "Did it have a happy ending?" I badly wanted him to say "yes" as a good omen for Sir John's luck today, but he didn't hear me and was soon lost to sight amongst the thickening crowd. I thought of Lady Eva and Isobel back at Walton and how they must be praying for a real-life happy ending to the tournament at Barham.

A group of squires I recognised from the feast were standing in a huddle nearby, discussing the joust. "This is a professional game now. You can be as chivalrous as you like, as brave and loyal as the next man, but these days it's jousting full-timers like Baldwin who win the prizes. Local amateurs don't stand a chance."

They glanced at me as I passed. One of them mentioned Sir John by name: "His arm was injured against the Scots, I heard. I don't think he can come back from that." He caught my eye.

"Hey, William De Combe. Is your knight entering the sword-fighting competition as well as the joust?" he asked. I said he wasn't, and Knobbly Head nodded his head as if that proved something important.

"Mmm, could be because of the arm trouble, and he's older than the rest too," he remarked, turning back to his friends. "He won't be champion again."

I slunk away fuming. My uncle may be older

ALLEYN'S SCHOOL LIBRARY

than some competitors but he has years of experience – how to hold the lance and how to balance his weight on a galloping horse. Surely that gives him a chance to win?

I said nothing of all this when I returned to our tent, and I tried to busy myself by laying out all the clothing we would need. Last night, Baldwin of Brandenburg's squires were boasting that he has got the very latest jousting armour – arm plates, newfangled gauntlets – all the newest stuff. "You've got to keep up with the trends," they said. Well, there's no getting away from the fact that Sir John's jousting equipment is old. But, fashionable or not, it's well-kept.
I've seen to that.

"All right, boy. Let's get ready," my uncle ordered. "There's to be all sorts of business before we start jousting – a parade, oath-taking, registering with the judges… We'd better get going and put this kit on now."

He stood in his undershirt and I combed his hair. Then, with my help, on went his leggings and leather shoes, leg plates and quilted coat. Next came the heavy mail shirt and the mail coif to cover his head, followed by his leather jerkin and the surcoat bearing his colours. I tried my hardest to make the dressing go smoothly, careful to avoid any signs of bad luck. Finally he slipped on his metal gauntlets and was ready for his helmet.

"Good, good," he murmured. "Now, boy. You stand at one end of the lists and hand me my lances. Adam, stand at the other end in case I need you…"

Don't say "if I fall"! Don't bring bad luck! I thought to myself in rising panic. Luckily Uncle didn't say it, but at that moment, with a flash of fear, I realised something. My happy ending, my whole quest, is now staked on my uncle and there's no going back. He is loyal, chivalrous, brave, a rescuer… but is he a champion?
If he wins I believe I will have found my true knight, made of real flesh and blood.

But what if he loses? I will have no tale to tell Isobel, except that I never found a true knight, that it an impossible dream and I shall therefore certainly never be one myself.

Bayard looked magnificent when we dressed

him in his flowing trappings and headgear. He sensed that action was near as soon as we saddled him up. My uncle has tied Lady Eleanor's scarf onto his helmet, where it will flutter alongside his heraldic crest.

I can hear the heralds summoning us to the lists. It is all or nothing now.

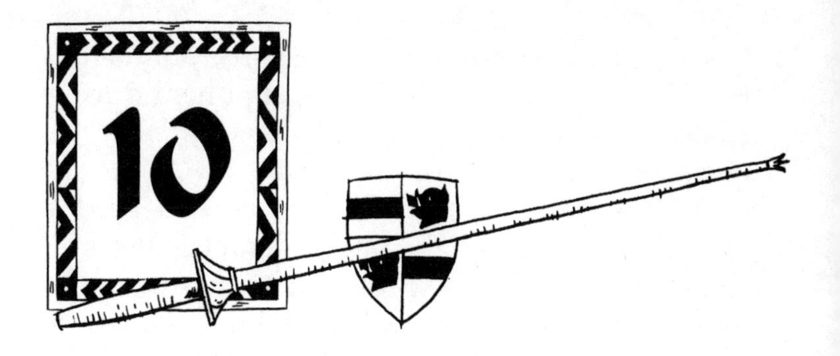

27 June 1332
Evening

It is the end of the first day's joust and I should sleep, but I can't because my head is so filled with noise and colour. When the knights paraded round the lists for the first time today the spectators roared so loudly that, if I listen carefully, I can still hear the sound ringing in my ears. A crowd of locals milled around behind the rails gawping at the nobles and their glittering ladies sitting in the main stand. When the judges were ready the rules were officially announced:

"In a bout each knight will ride eight times against his opponent. The overall winner on points will go forward to the next bout.

Three points will be awarded for unhorsing your opponent. Three points will be given for breaking your lance by hitting it on the tip of your opponent's lance."

"That'd be a good shot!" Adam remarked as we stood listening.

"Three points for striking your opponent's

visor three times during a bout. Three points for breaking more lances than your opponent during a bout. One point for breaking a lance on an opponent's shield."

For the hundredth time I nervously checked the breakable tips on the bunch of lances I was carrying, hoping they would shatter easily and score points for my uncle. Meanwhile he lifted his arm and waved as he paraded round with the others. When the crowd roared back I realised he was deliberately waving the arm that had healed, so they could see it was completely well again.

"A knight will be disqualified for striking an opponent's horse, striking a man with his back turned or taking off his own helmet more than once during a bout," the rules continued.

Then there were more rituals, such as bowing to the ladies in the stand and arranging who was to fight whom. Sir John took the opportunity to slip off his helmet and call for a drink. I ran over with a cup of water and saw that he looked hot.

"God preserve us, I'd rather joust in January," he complained, just as the French champion Geoffrey of Ardres rode by. "Worn out already, old man?" he taunted. He is certainly not always chivalrous.

There were sword-fighting bouts to begin with. The crowd gradually worked itself up to ever-louder cheering. While we watched, one of Baldwin's squires sidled up to me. "The joust is ours," he hissed. "I wouldn't wager on it," I snapped back.

"Oh, but I already have," he sneered. "If your man comes up against Baldwin, he'll have no chance. A famous young champion against a creaky old local? No contest!" he laughed. "I'd better get into position. My knight is up first. Find me at the end and I'll buy you a pie with my winnings. It's my duty to help the poor, after all." I wanted to trip the little bragger up as he swaggered away.

"Champion of many jousts, Baldwin of Brandenburg!" a herald announced. The crowd whooped at the sight of him. He was wearing a red surcoat and a magnificent model of a black hawk was fixed on top of his helm. He rode across to the main stand and bowed. Then he began his first bout.

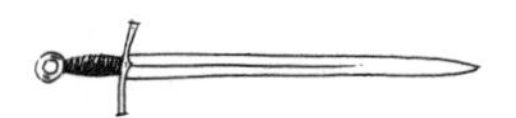

"Hurrah!" the crowd erupted as his lance shattered on his opponent's shield. "Hurrah!" they shouted louder as he turned, rode again and struck his opponent's visor. Baldwin was in another class, and before long the other rider had been tipped off his horse into the dusty straw.

"Baldwin's good, very good," Adam remarked in a worried tone. Other contestants rode against each other until, at last, it was Sir

John's turn. I handed him a lance; he spurred Bayard forward and I prayed. He scored well and beat his opponent easily enough, though not

as stylishly as Baldwin, or even Geoffrey of Ardres. But he got through to tomorrow's round so we live to fight another day.

28 June 1332

Once more Sir John prevailed and got through to the last four, to ride on the final day tomorrow. He has shattered so many lances I am afraid we will run out, but he says that Piers De Montald will give him some more since he rides on his behalf. Luckily Uncle only has bruises. But I saw one knight with serious wounds being carried off the field by his squires.

I must tend to the armour again tonight, while Adam looks after Bayard. I've noticed that other contestants have more than one warhorse, but he is our only chance.

Tomorrow there will be an overall winner. I must dress Uncle with even more care. It's all I can do to help him.

29 June 1332

Afternoon

I am making some hasty notes before my uncle rides again. Baldwin of Brandenburg has got through to the final. The next bout will be Geoffrey of Ardres versus Sir John De Walton. I must go and prepare and pray hard.

Sir Geoffrey fell to the ground with a satisfying thump. I am spattered with mud and grime but I don't care! My uncle is through to the final.

An account of the Barham Castle jousting final, written for Isobel De Walton, 1332.

Baldwin of Brandenburg
versus
Sir John De Walton

Ride one: Score equal. Both lances smashed on shields. Score: one all.

Ride two: Sir John strikes Baldwin's visor. A hit! Score still equal.

Ride three: No score.

Ride four: No score. The crowd wants more.

Ride five: Baldwin strikes Sir John's visor!
Score is equal still.

Ride six: Baldwin breaks a lance and Sir John does not.
Score: two/one.

Ride seven: Baldwin breaks another lance.
Score: three/one. Time is running out.

Ride eight: Sir John De Walton unseats Baldwin of Brandenburg, and breaks his own lance, too!
Final score: three/five.

—Glorious winner: Sir John De Walton!

30 June 1332

I am the squire of the truest knight there ever was. To the cheers of the crowd yesterday my uncle received the prize from Lady Eleanor, a beautiful pot full of gold coins. They will buy new armour, a new warhorse as companion to Bayard, and there will still be plenty left over.

Later I saw my juggling friend again. "A happy ending for you!" he cried. I thought of buying a pie and giving it to Baldwin's rude squire, but I decided that wouldn't be chivalrous of me.

Later we went to the castle for more feasting and dancing. There, inevitably, I ran into Lady Anne again. But this time she didn't take any notice of me and concentrated her attentions on Geoffrey of Ardres. "He's a widower with lots of land back home. He might make a good marriage for Lady Anne," Sir John remarked. For Geoffrey's sake I hope he writes poetry and has a thick skin.

I am longing to get back to Walton to tell cousin Isobel what happened and see Lady Eva's face when she knows for sure that we are all safe.

5 JULY 1332
WALTON

I am writing in the stables at Walton again. I can hear Bayard gently swishing his tail. Adam is outside cleaning some muddy boots in the yard and in the background someone is singing.
I think it is Isobel's voice:

Dance for my lady,
Dance for my lord…

I am glad to be back at Walton. It's a place where I know what to expect.

When my diary is ended I shall seek permission to ride over to Copthorne Priory, where they keep many manuscripts safe in their library. My little one can hide among them. Perhaps one day it will be read by others. I shall call it *The Tale of the True Knight,* but first I must finish it by writing of our journey home.

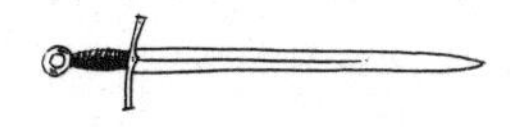

We left Barham Castle swiftly after the tournament, despite Piers De Montald's invitation to stay a while. As much as he likes jousting it seemed that this time Sir John wanted nothing more than to get home. Adam mentioned it as we saddled up the horses.

"He has proved he can still win. I think that might be enough for him."

"What? You mean he might not fight again?" I asked. Adam laughed. "Who knows? It may be your turn next," he said. "I reckon you should start practising your jousting, William De Combe."

Piers De Montald spoke to us, as courteous and suave as ever, before we left. "I shall see you again soon, I hope, Sir John. Perhaps next time your nephew here will be ready for knighting,"

"He will be as true a knight as any there ever was," my uncle replied. I felt a surge of excitement and pride.

We stayed one night in the inn at Totbury and while we were there I asked about the travelling friar.

"Him? That cheating troublemaker!" the landlord spat out. "He got drunk in the street one day and insulted all the lords, the earls and finally the king before he was taken off." I was shocked to hear that someone could so far forget themselves, and imagine he might be hanged for it.

We rode on hard to Copthorne and the prior there wisely said nothing about jousts and crusades but gladly accepted some of Sir John's prize money in return for saying daily prayers for his soul. Then we rode on to Walton and when we clip-clopped through the manor gates the relief on Lady Eva's face was plain to see. Meanwhile Isobel danced round us, positively yelping with delight.

Sir John answered their questions good-heartedly: "Of course I won! Hold your hand out." He grinned and pressed gold coins into their open palms.

"Who did you beat? How did you score?" Isobel demanded, but Uncle just waved her questions away and turned to Lady Eva. "Never mind all that now. William will tell you the tale. What I want to know is whether the hay-making went smoothly and did you get the roof repaired without trouble?" he asked.

"Of course I did! Hold your hand out," Lady Eva replied and when he did so she lifted it to her lips and kissed it.

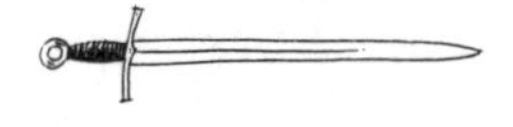

As soon as she could, Isobel met up with me in the solar. "Sit comfortably and I shall tell you the tale of my quest," I announced grandly. She looked on excitedly as I smoothed my diary parchments out on my knee. "Did you find a true knight?" she demanded.

"I have learnt there is no such thing as the

kind of true knight found in stories," I said. Her face was a picture of disappointment, and I felt mean that I had let her feel that way for even a second. "Instead I found a real live true knight," I grinned, "one who is brave, loyal, chivalrous and a champion, but who is also human. He is kind and honest and understands how the world works, and he helped to teach me," I grinned.

"Oh, what was his name?" she asked eagerly. "I should dearly like to meet such a knight!"

"Your father, Sir John De Walton!" I replied. To my pleasure she laughed with delight.

"Our hero was beside us all the time, while we had our noses in books," I laughed along with her.

"And you, William. Now you have found the truth, will you be a true knight, too?" she asked.

"My lady," I replied in a grand tone, and bowed down low.

"I hope you will be my true knight, William," she murmured, and I was glad that my face was down in a bow, because my cheeks flushed hot.

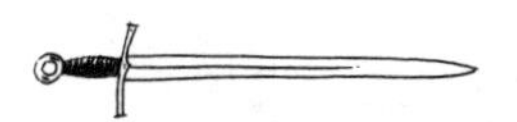

Now, two days later, we are about halfway through reading the diary, halfway because she keeps interrupting with questions. I am going to carry on the reading after supper today, but now I must finish the writing, or it will be like some magical never-ending story and I shall find myself reading it to Isobel forever.

She and I will both want to start a new story soon.

Fact File

Medieval England After 1332

The time that historians call "medieval" covers a little over 400 years from 1066 to 1500. William De Combe lived during a small part of this period, in the reign of King Edward III. It was a time when great upheavals were about to change people's lives forever.

The Black Death

At the time of this story England had a population of about three-and-a-half million people. But then the plague, called the Black Death, struck in 1348. By the end of the deadly epidemic the population had fallen by up to a third. Whole villages were wiped out and William would have been lucky to survive.

Changes in Feudal Life

The Black Death had a big effect on the way that society was organised. In William's boyhood people rented land from their lord in return for giving him regular service, such as fighting for him or working in his fields. After the Black Death so many people had died that there weren't enough people to make the old system work. Those peasants that survived began to be paid for their work. The king had to pay soldiers in his army rather than just summoning subjects to fight. Once William became a knight he might have been paid by the king to fight in the Hundred Years War against France, which began in 1340.

Becoming a Knight

When he was about 21 William would become a knight. He would have to fast (not eat) for two days and then spend a night praying in the chapel. The next morning he would bathe and put on a white tunic under his armour. His lord would tap him on the shoulder with a sword and give him some spurs. After he was knighted his title would be "Sir". William would have married someone from his own social rank, quite possibly his cousin.

Chivalry

During Edward III's reign, the idea of a chivalrous "true knight" was a very popular one. There were lots of stories told about knightly adventures involving magic, ladies, dragons and enchantment. The king encouraged his knights to act out this idea of chivalry at jousting tournaments. These were held often; the most skilful knights were invited from abroad to compete against local champions.

Medieval Towns

In William's time towns were gradually developing and people began to move to them.

Medieval town houses were long and narrow, because of lack of space. The ground floor was often used as a shop. The upper storey overhung the street to give the inhabitants a bit more room upstairs. Only the very rich had stone houses. Ordinary houses were wooden-framed, and the space in between the frames was filled with a mixture of clay, dung and straw called daub, packed onto a framework of wooden sticks called wattle. Inside such a house there was very little privacy and there were no toilets; only buckets or chamber pots that had to be emptied outside.

Poor people slept on bags filled with rushes or heather, called pallettes. Only rich people had proper wooden beds. Domestic animals, such as pigs and chickens, often ran freely in the town streets.

Street Names

Modern streets in old towns often have medieval names to this day. You might, for instance, see "The Shambles", which in medieval times meant that butchers lived in the street. Towns sometimes had walls surrounding them, with entrances called gates. Look out for modern roads with the word "gate" in their name, such as "Northgate" or "Southgate".

Medieval Villages

In medieval villages poor people lived in small hovels with one room, perhaps divided by a partition to make a sleeping area and a living area. There wouldn't be a chimney, only a hole in the roof to let the smoke from the central fire out.

Jousting

Jousting tournaments had strict rules and regulations set out by the king. Some knights, such as Baldwin of Brandenburg, were professional jousters, travelling Europe to fight for money. Others, such as Sir John, would joust if asked by his lord or king. The earliest jousts, called melées, consisted of two teams of knights all fighting at the same time, as if they were on a battlefield. Because this type of joust was so dangerous, however, it was banned and individual jousting came into fashion.

Glossary

Here are some explanations of medieval words from William's story.

Chain mail

Armour made from lots of small interlinking metal rings.

Crusades

Medieval wars fought between Christians and Muslims. They were an attempt by Christians to control Jerusalem and the Holy Land.

Feudalism

The arrangement where people were given land and in return they worked regularly for their landlord.

Freeman

Someone who rented land but was free to move from one estate to another.

Great Hall

A large grand room where a lord and his household met and ate.

Joust

A tournament which only knights could enter. They rode against each other, trying to score hits with their lances.

Keep

A large tower-like building containing the most important rooms in a castle.

Knight

A noble who has been given the title of knight by his lord. In return, he had to fight for his lord if requested to do so.

Lance

A long pointed spear.

Manor

A farm estate with a village and a manor house on it.

Page

A boy of noble birth training to be a squire.

Priory

A settlement of monks, led by a prior.

Solar

The lord's private rooms in the castle where he and his family lived

Villein

A peasant who was not allowed to leave the estate where he or she was born without their lord's permission.

Other titles in this series

The diary of a Young Roman Soldier
Marcus Gallo travels to Britain with his legion to help pacify the wild Celtic tribes.

The diary of a Young Tudor Lady-in Waiting
Young Rebecca Swann joins her aunt as a lady-in-waiting to Queen Elizabeth the First.

The Diary of a Young Nurse in World War II
Jean Harris is hired to train as a nurse in a London hospital just as World War II breaks out.

The diary of a Young West Indian Immigrant
It is 1961 and Gloria Charles travels from Dominica to Britain to start a new life.

The diary of a 1960s Teenager
Teenager Jane Leachman is offered a job working in swinging London's fashion industry.

The diary of a Young Roman Girl
It is AD74 and Secundia Fulvia Popillia is helping her family prepare for her sister's wedding.

The diary of Samuel Pepys's Clerk
It is 1665 and young Roger Scratch travels to London to work for his kinsman Pepys.

The diary of a World War II Pilot
It is 1938 and young Johnny Hedley joins up to become a pilot in Britain's Royal Air Force.

ALLEYN'S SCHOOL LIBRARY